The Kis

"I need to k   died from," Scully insisted.

"Please," Osborne begged, no longer threatening. "The bodies shouldn't be exposed."

"Do all the victims have these boils?" Scully demanded.

Osborne paid no attention. He set about wrapping the plastic back around Bobby Torrence.

Scully refused to be ignored. As Osborne bent over the corpse, she leaned down to say into Osborne's ear, "You're burning the bodies. *Why?*"

Still Osborne ignored her, as he reached forward to get the last piece of plastic over Bobby's boil-covered face.

As he leaned over, the biggest boil on the dead man's face exploded.

Yellow pus shot up. It hit Osborne, and splattered across his forehead.

**Read all of the X-Files
Young Adult books:**

Quarantine

A novelization by Les Martin
Based on the television series

THE X FILES™

created by Chris Carter
Based on the teleplay
written by Chris Carter
and Howard Gordon

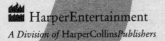
HarperEntertainment
A Division of HarperCollins Publishers

Based on the episode "F. Emasculata,"
by Chris Carter and Howard Gordon

ISBN 0-06-447189-6

HarperCollins®, 🕮®, and HarperEntertainment™
are registered trademarks of HarperCollins Publishers Inc.

First Edition, 1999

Visit HarperEntertainment on the World Wide Web at
http://www.harpercollins.com

Chapter One

The vultures circled overhead in the hot blue sky. Big, dark birds with wide wings, scarlet heads, glittering eyes, and cruel beaks.

Dr. Robert Torrence watched them through the trees of the Costa Rican rain forest. As a biologist, he was used to wildlife. But these vultures gave him the creeps. It wasn't only their looks, it was their smarts. They knew what they were doing. They lived on the flesh of the dead, and somewhere close by they sensed dinnertime approaching.

Dr. Torrence forced himself to stop looking at them and got back to what he was doing. With a wooden tongue depressor he pried a piece of loose bark from a tree. Underneath he spied a large black beetle.

"Come to Papa," he said under his breath.

Slowly he extended another tongue depressor so as not to scare the bug. After a moment's hesitation, the beetle scurried onto the stick. Dr. Torrence quickly moved it to a clear plastic container in a metal carrying case and dropped the bug inside. Before it could escape, Dr. Torrence slid the top of the compartment closed. He did a quick count. Seventeen specimens.

"Enough for today," Dr. Torrence told himself. He snapped the carrying case shut and wiped sweat from his metal-framed glasses. He scratched the five-day-old beard on his face. What he would do for a shave and hot shower—yet both were three days and two hundred miles away.

Dr. Torrence loaded up his oversized backpack and shouldered it. But before he could start the trek back to his base camp, he heard earsplitting squawking.

He recognized the sound even before he spotted the flock of vultures coming down through the treetops.

There was a feast of death going on nearby.

Dr. Torrence might be bone-weary, but

he could not resist taking a look. Studying animal life was not just his profession, it was his passion.

It was easy to find what he was looking for. Vultures made a lot of noise when they were enjoying themselves.

He saw at least twenty of them in a clearing, voraciously ripping apart a carcass with their beaks.

"Shoo! Go away! Shoo!" Dr. Torrence shouted, waving his hands as he moved forward.

With angry cries, the large birds scattered into the air. They did not fly far, however, settling nearby on low hanging branches, as though assuming a deathwatch.

He slipped off his backpack and squatted next to what was left of a large dead boar. While the sight would have turned most people's stomachs, it merely stirred Dr. Torrence's curiosity.

The wild boar was one of the toughest of animals, he knew. You could shoot a charging boar between the eyes and it would keep on coming. What had killed this one?

He peered at its ripped flesh. At first glance

he saw only that the vultures had done a good job of tearing it to ribbons. Then he saw something that made him look closer.

Among the open wounds were angry red boils, swelling like balloons. They pulsed in and out, as if they had hearts of their own. Dr. Torrence had seen boils before—but never ones as nasty as these.

Even more interesting, large red-orange beetles were crawling around the boils.

Still squatting, he reached into his backpack and removed his sample case. Then he pulled a pair of latex gloves out of a side pocket and slipped them on.

A moment later, he had one of the beetles stowed in a plastic compartment. Then Dr. Torrence turned back to the carcass.

The boils were gigantic. And they seemed to get even bigger as he watched, their membranes stretching as they pulsed. With one gloved finger, he gently touched the boil nearest to him.

"Ugghhh!" Dr. Torrence grunted as the boil burst, spraying pus across his glasses and into his mouth. Grimacing with disgust, he spit out the foul substance, wiped his lenses on his shirt, and put the glasses back on. He looked at the wound that the boil had left behind—and decided he had seen enough for the moment. He would learn more when he got out of the forest and back to the lab.

But later that evening he was too woozy to capture more than a handful of specimens in the forest. By the time he dragged himself back to his campsite, he was soaked with sweat, despite the evening chill.

Stumbling into his tent he got into his sleeping bag and lay there shivering, then sweating.

His mind fought the waves of darkness that flowed over it. He knew he had to force himself out of his sleeping bag. He had to get to his radio transmitter if it was the last thing he did.

The way he felt, it might be.

He crawled out of his tent, playing the beam of his flashlight ahead of him. He spotted the radio propped against a log near the dying campfire. He turned on the power and adjusted the frequency. Clearing his throat, he spoke as loudly as he coould into the mike. His voice was little more than a croak": "BDP Field Base, come in please."

No answer.

He decided to wait a moment, then try again.

His face was on fire. His hand went to it and felt the burning hot boils all over it.

He grabbed the mike weakly and took a deep breath. Desperately he gasped out, "This is Dr. Robert Torrence from the Biodiversity Project. I am requesting immediate evacuation from sector zee-one-five."

He paused. He had run out of breath. He sucked air and managed to say, "This is a medical emergency. Repeat. A medical emergency. *Please respond.*"

Torrence struggled to repeat the message but it was no use. He fell back and stared up at the cold moon as he listened to the static of the empty airwaves.

The last picture in his mind's eye was of vultures circling overhead.

Just seven hours later Filipo Garcia was leading a squad of Costa Rican Rangers with weapons at the ready, when he heard the vultures squawking among the trees.

"Stop a second," he ordered his men in Spanish. "You hear that?"

Garcia was no biologist, but he had grown up in the rain forest. He knew the sound and what it meant.

So did his men. They asked no questions when he directed them to the source. "Come on, let's try over there."

As the men entered the clearing, Garcia let off a shot.

The flock of vultures on the ground scattered into the air, revealing a pair of legs amidst a buzzing cloud of insects.

Garcia waved the insects away and looked down at the body.

Was this the Yankee scientist they had

been ordered to find and helicopter out?

There wasn't enough of the man's face left to tell for sure. Just a pair of metal-framed glasses, their lenses cracked by the vultures' pitiless beaks, and a swarm of large red-orange beetles crawling around them.

Chapter Two

The Cumberland State Correctional Facility was not built for comfort. A double razor wire fence surrounded its high walls and guard towers. Inside, stark hallways ran past rows of steel doors. Behind the doors were tiny cells, more of which were for solitary confinement than in most prisons. The State of Virginia sent its hard-core criminals to Cumberland, where they paid their debt to society in full—with interest added on.

Darnell Winston had been a guard at Cumberland for a year. Long enough to get to know the prisoners—but not long enough to lose compassion for them. He felt for a guy like Bobby Torrence. Even if you were as ugly and nasty as Bobby, it was tough to be alone in a cell day after day, night after night, with nothing else to look forward to for the rest of your life.

Winston didn't mind going out of his way to deliver a package for Bobby. It might even brighten his day a bit.

Winston should have known better.

Bobby didn't bother getting up from his bunk when Winston shouted through a slot in the cell door, "Hey Bobby, you got mail. Maybe someone's sending you some kind of present."

"Don't waste my time, Winston," Bobby growled. He sat staring gloomily at nothing. "Both of us know I ain't got nobody."

"It might be from that religious charity down in Annandale," Winston said. "I hear they've been sending fruitcakes."

When Bobby didn't answer, Winston shrugged. He shoved the package through the slot and walked away.

Some people you just can't help, Winston thought. He was learning why other guards laughed when he worried about the prisoners.

Bobby stared dully at the package on his

cell floor. Finally he worked up enough interest to go pick it up.

The outside of the package did not tell him much. The return address was too smudged to read in the dim light. The parcel had gone to other addresses before the delivery service tracked him down here, but each was crossed out. Only his name was clear: *Robert Torrence*.

Bobby ripped open the package. He pulled out something about the size of his heavily tattooed forearm, wrapped in newspaper. He tried to read the paper, but it was in Spanish. He shook his head.

"What the . . ." Peeling off the newspaper, he gasped.

"Ugghhh!"

He was holding a pig's leg, severed at the thigh.

He dropped it like a hot coal. Then he kicked it as far away as he could, which was not very far. It bounced against the cell wall and lay on the floor less than five feet away.

Bobby pressed his face against the cell door and screamed, "Hey, Winston, you think it's funny? What kinda stuff you trying to pull here?"

He waited. No answer. No footsteps coming. Taking a deep breath, he shouted, "*Get this thing outta my crib!*"

Again no answer.

Winston would not be back until breakfast time—ten long hours away.

Bobby went to his bunk, lay down, and closed his eyes. Sleep was the only way to make the time pass.

But sleep wouldn't come. His eyes kept opening, no matter how hard he tried to keep them shut. He didn't want to look at that hideous pig's leg—but he had to.

When he finally gave in and looked at the leg, his eyes widened.

He peered at it more intently. Parts of the leg had turned red and blotchy. Inside those red blotches, nasty boils were swelling.

He got up to take a closer look.

It looked as though the boils were throbbing, pulsating.

Not believing his eyes, Bobby leaned over the leg for an even better look.

He would never know what a big mistake that was.

The two men who examined him the next day, however, did.

Osbourne and Auerback wore protective decontamination suits that covered them from head to toe. Clear Plastic masks protected their faces. They looked like a pair of astronauts as they bent over Bobby, writhing and sweating on an examination table. A high-intensity light clearly illuminated the red boils all over his body.

"When was he exposed?" Osborne asked.

"Eighteen hours ago," Auerbach replied.

Osborne shook his head in surprise. "I've never heard of anything developing so quickly. Not even *this*."

Bobby groaned as he squinted up into the painful light.

Dimly, he made out the men bent over him. What was going on? What was wrong with him?

He managed to gasp out, "Where's the prison doc?"

The two men ignored his words as one of them

measured the size of a boil.

Bobby's tongue felt as though it weighed a ton, but still he raised his voice. *"I want to see the prison doc!"*

"Don't worry," Auerbach soothed him. "We're specialists, Mr. Torrence."

Osborne finished taking a measurement. "Five centimeters," he told Auerbach, who wrote the figure down. "The boils seem fairly uniform in size."

"What's his basal temperature?" Auerbach asked, his pen poised.

"One-oh-three point five."

"Up a degree in the past hour," Auerbach noted. "We'll check it again in ten minutes if—"

"Yeah, if—though that looks unlikely," Osborne said. He checked a meter hooked up to a device that covered Bobby Torrence's nose. "Oxygen saturation is eighty-two percent."

"Jesus! What's wrong with me?" Bobby cried, straining at the straps that held him to the table.

"Try and relax, Mr. Torrence. We're here to help you," Auerbach said, sticking a needle into Bobby's arm.

Chapter Three

Winston rocked on his heels as he watched two prisoners clean out Torrence's cell. He felt bad about what happened to Bobby Torrence. He would not have felt that way if it had happened to these two, Paul Zimmer or Steve Tyson. As far as Winston was concerned, nothing was too bad for Paul and Steve.

With his brutish physique and permanent sneer, Paul made his attitude known before he even opened his mouth. His long hair and beard made him look even meaner.

Steve was thin and wiry, with a five o'clock shadow stubbling his face. He was Paul's buddy, and just as nasty. Paul, though, was smarter—which wasn't saying much. Still, it made Paul Steve's hero. Steve followed where Paul led—and that was usually toward violence.

They had a reputation at Cumberland. Even other hardened criminals stayed out of their way. Winston kept a safe distance and a hand near his pistol holster when he ordered them into Bobby's old cell.

It wasn't just the two men that kept Winston outside the cell, though. It was Winston who had found Bobby writhing on the floor. He didn't want to get close to whatever might still be there. He remembered how Bobby looked with those fiery, pulsating boils. He knew he would keep seeing those boils in his nightmares.

Winston barked at the two convicts through the open cell door.

"Stick every piece of bedding, every piece of clothing, in the laundry bin," he ordered them. "Don't miss anything. Not a pillow. Not a handkerchief. And make sure you shut the bin tight before you roll it out of the cell. I'll be back in five minutes. I expect you to be finished."

"Okay, we'll be here," Paul shouted, as Winston headed down the corridor.

Paul turned to Steve, who was stuffing a mattress cover into a big yellow plastic laundry bin on wheels.

"You see that?" Paul remarked quietly. "Like he couldn't clear out of here fast enough."

Steve frowned. "Weird, like everything else lately. The whole cell block is empty."

Paul nodded. "Yeah. And McGuire says they're full up at the infirmary. They're bringing in more beds."

Steve thought for a second. "Maybe there's something going around."

Paul gave Steve a look. Steve was okay, a good pal. You needed a pal in the slammer, somebody to watch your back. But there was no denying Steve's brain left something to be desired. It was lucky that Paul could do the thinking for both of them.

"Yeah, something going around," Paul said. "I guess you could say that."

"Hey, you know something about what's happening?" Steve asked. Leave it to Paul, he thought. Paul was always in the know.

"I know that these sheets and stuff are

not going to the laundry," Paul said.

Steve wrinkled his brow. "What do you mean?"

Paul could have waited for Steve to figure it. But he didn't have that much time.

"McGuire said they're going to some kind of incinerator."

"No laundry?" replied Steve, sounding concerned. Suddenly a light bulb went on in his head. "But the regular laundry pickup is still happening," he said with a smile.

Paul nodded. Steve had finally caught on to the plan he had in mind.

Chapter Four

FBI Special Agent Dana Scully could tell when her partner, Special Agent Fox Mulder, was teed off.

Mulder did not have to say anything, and usually didn't. His eyes just got a little darker. His jaws clenched.

Scully saw that Mulder was fuming at the moment. This assignment wasn't exactly up his alley. There were more important things Mulder wanted to investigate in the world—and beyond it. Yet orders were orders. And Mulder was a pro, as was Scully.

The guard at the entrance of the Cumberland State Correctional Facility Checked their badges, then he make a phone call. He talked for several minutes, careful not to let Mulder and Scully overhear.

The two agents exchanged glances. There was something unusual going on. This man was not your typical prison guard. He wore a National Guard uniform, complete with helmet and sidearm, and his semiautomatic was in easy reach.

Two other armed soldiers appeared.

The guard handed Scully and Mulder back their badges.

"These men will accompany you inside," the guard instructed.

One soldier led the way into the prison. The other followed behind Mulder and Scully. Their footsteps echoed though empty corridors and up and down iron stairways. They went through one clanging steel door after another without seeing a soul, but the soldiers kept weapons at the ready.

"What information do we have, Scully?" Mulder asked. "I didn't get much. Just to meet you here. I was told you would fill me in."

"I received only the barest facts," Scully said. "According to my briefing, the two prisoners escaped by hiding in a laundry cart."

"The guards must not have watched enough prison escape movies," cracked Mulder.

Scully's face remained serious. "Both men who escaped were serving life sentences. They were killers. Violent killers."

Their conversation stopped abruptly as the soldier in front halted them with an upraised hand. He picked up a phone beside a closed door and punched in a number.

"The two FBI agents are here," he reported.

He listened for a moment, then said, "Yes, sir."

The soldier opened the door and stepped aside. "You can go in."

The two soldiers followed Mulder and Scully through the door with their hands on their weapons.

The room Scully and Mulder entered was large, square, and empty. On each side a windowed steel door led off to a corridor.

Mulder glanced through one of the door windows. Instantly, he motioned for Scully to take a look.

She did. What she saw on the other side of the door were two men in protective white suits and headgear, wheeling a lab table loaded with medical equipment into a room off the corridor.

"I thought this was about escaped prisoners," Mulder said.

"It is," Scully informed him.

"Then who are the men in the funny suits?" Mulder wanted to know.

"I don't know," Scully commented. "It looks to me like some kind of decontamination situation. A chemical spill, perhaps, or an asbestos problem, or maybe an infectious disease. That's as much as I can—"

She stopped as a door on the opposite side of the room opened. Men poured through it.

There were at least fifteen of them. All wore navy blue windbreakers with U.S. MARSHAL on the front and back in big gold letters.

One federal marshal confronted Scully and Mulder with a hard look. His voice was even harder. "FBI?"

"That's right," Mulder replied.

"What's the matter, the bureau run out of crooked politicians to sting?" the marshal asked coldly.

"Excuse me?" Mulder said in mock surprise, raising his eyebrows. He knew from experience that the FBI often provoked different feelings in people—feelings that were not exactly warm.

One of the soldiers handed the marshal a piece of paper. Glancing at it, he looked at the special agents again. "Mulder and Scully?" he asked.

"That's right," Scully answered in a voice just as frigid. "And you are?"

"Tapia," he answered. He did not seem to like saying even that much.

"We have official orders to work with the federal marshals on this manhunt," Scully informed him.

"Either of you ever run an escaped convict operation?" Tapia demanded.

"No," said Mulder.

"Then you'd be a big help if you just

tried to stay out of the way," Tapia advised them. His contempt was clear.

With that, he turned away. His body language plainly showed he did not want anything more to do with them.

Mulder's voice was cutting. "We'd be happy to do that. But first we'd like to talk to someone in charge."

Tapia's back stiffened. He wheeled around to face Mulder. "I'm in charge here," he snapped.

"Apparently not," Mulder said icily. "Or you'd know why our involvement was requested."

Scully stepped in, trying to defuse the situation.

"We're really not sure why we've been called in here," she said gently. "Perhaps we would do best to speak with the warden or someone who—"

Tapia cut her off. "No one's here. The prison's been taken over by the National Guard. They've closed off most of the facility."

"Why?" Scully asked.

"I don't know why," Tapia replied impatiently. "Federal marshal's business isn't in here. It's outside, trying to catch those two convicts."

Then he turned and quickly strode away.

Scully and Mulder watched Tapia lead his marshals out another door. The soldiers followed, leaving Scully and Mulder by themselves.

"Where did this assignment originate, Scully?" Mulder asked.

"It came out of Skinner's office," she replied.

"Did he say anything about why he gave it to us?" Mulder asked.

"No," Scully said. "Why?"

"This isn't the kind of thing the FBI usually gets called in on."

He turned back to the door window. Scully stood behind him, looking over his shoulder.

Both of them saw the decontamination team again. The men were wheeling another lab table into a room. Mulder couldn't be sure, but he thought he saw a body on it.

"I've got a feeling we're not being told the entire story here," he said.

"I have to agree." Scully nodded her head.

Mulder turned to Scully. "You think you can get in there and find out what's going on?"

"I can try," Scully offered.

Mulder nodded, and started to move off.

"Where are you going?" Scully wanted to know.

Mulder paused long enough to say, "To see if I can get in Tapia's way."

Chapter Five

Mulder caught up with Tapia and his men as they were leaving the prison.

"Mind if I tag along with you?" Mulder asked the stone-faced marshal.

"I can't see how I can stop you," Tapia replied. "You apparently have authorization."

"I'd appreciate any pointers you can give me about this kind of operation," Mulder said blandly, as if Tapia had given him the warmest of welcomes.

"I don't have time to give on-the-job training," Tapia said sharply. "Those two men out there are natural-born killers. Walking time-bombs. Every minute they're free is a minute that a murder can occur."

Tapia stopped suddenly. "Look, Agent Mulder," he snapped. "I'll give you a run-down, short and sweet. After that, you'll have to just keep your mouth shut and your eyes open."

"Right," said Mulder. "I'm all ears."

"On a manhunt like this," said Tapia, "all we can do at first is to search the area around the prison in widening circles. But we don't really expect to find the escapees that way, unless we have a stroke of luck. With characters like these two, we have to wait for the first reports to come in from local police to pick up the trail."

"Reports of what?" Mulder asked.

"Guess," Tapia answered bluntly.

"I have to go!" pleaded seven-year-old Ellen Tracy.

"Me too!" announced her five-year-old sister, Alice.

Robert Tracy, at the wheel of the family mobile home, spoke to them sternly. "Kids, I asked you just twenty minutes ago, right before we left the trailer camp."

The girls were not frightened. They knew that underneath his gruff manner, their daddy was a big softy.

"But I gotta," Ellen proclaimed.

"Me too," echoed Alice.

"Honey, let's not spoil the end of a wonderful week with a family fight," Robert's wife, Anne, chimed in. "Look, there's a rest area. We can pull over for a minute, then be on our way."

"Okay, you win," Robert grumbled. He pulled the big white mobile home off the highway and parked it in front of a low stone building with a sign that read: BEAR CREEK STATE PARK TOURIST CENTER.

The girls ran out of the vehicle as soon as it came to a stop. Their mother followed them, and then Robert climbed out.

"I might as well go, too," he said. "We've got a long drive if we want to get home before night. Let's not waste time now. Okay, girls?"

Robert watched his wife and kids go to the ladies' room on the right side of the building. Then he hustled off to the men's room on the left.

Inside, he headed for the urinal against the wall. He was alone in the men's room.

Or so he thought.

Robert did not hear the stall door swing open behind his back.

He never knew what hit him.

Even if he had, it wouldn't have helped.

Paul Zimmer was as strong as a bull and as savage as a tiger.

Steve Tyson, coming out from behind the far side of the stall, was too late to join in the action. All he could do was catch the wallet Paul tossed him just as Paul dangled a set of car keys triumphantly in the air.

Anne Tracy got a far better look at the two men than her husband had.

Herding her daughters out of the ladies' room, she saw their mobile home roar past them, heading for the highway.

No! Why is he leaving without us? she thought in sudden panic.

The little girls stared openmouthed.

As the vehicle careened around a corner, Anne caught a glimpse of the two men inside. The big one with the beard was at the wheel, his long hair whipping in the wind.

The other shouted out the window as the mobile home drove away.

Anne gasped. "Robert!"

She ran to see if he was still in the men's room.

He was.

Somehow she found the strength to call the police from a pay phone before she put her arms around her children.

"Don't cry, don't cry," she told them, even as tears streamed down her face.

The cell phone in Chief Marshal Tapia's pocket buzzed.

Mulder watched as Tapia pulled it out. The marshal listened a minute, then clicked it off.

From the look on Tapia's face, Mulder knew what the marshal was going to say before he said it.

"The first victim," Tapia announced in a grim tone.

Chapter Six

Mulder looked down at the body on the floor of the rest room. The back of the dead man's head was caved in. A dried pool of blood lay like spilled paint on the white tile.

"Chances are the murder weapon was a rock," Tapia explained. "My guess is we'll find it nearby."

"A rock with a lot of muscle behind it," Mulder noted. "But I doubt the muscle is still nearby."

"Seen enough?" asked Tapia.

Mulder gave one more look, then nodded.

"Time to quiz the widow, then," Tapia said, and led the way out.

Mulder knew the interview would be difficult. He had seen the weeping woman and two scared little girls in front of the rest stop when he arrived with the marshals in their swarm of official cars. She had barely managed to point to the men's room while her body shook with sobs.

Inside the prison, Scully peered through the door window.

The decontamination team had vanished into another room. But Scully spotted a man coming down the corridor. He wore a doctor's white lab coat. Below the hem she saw the pants of a dark blue suit.

Scully banged on the door.

Startled, the man looked at her. He started to turn away, back to where he came from.

Scully pounded harder. The man could not pretend not to hear it.

Reluctantly, he came to the door. His face was pale and timid as he stared at Scully through the window. She shoved her badge in front of his watery blue eyes.

"I'm sorry," he said through the glass. "This is a restricted area."

"Who are you?" Scully demanded.

"Dr. Osborne," he told her. He sounded as if he would have liked to be anywhere in the world but here.

"Are you the prison doctor?" Scully wanted to know.

"No."

"Who do you work for?" Scully asked.

Osborne hestitated, then answered, "The CDC."

"You work for the Centers for Disease Control?" said Scully. "What are you doing in here?"

Osborne did not answer. Instead he began to turn away. He froze when Scully banged on the door, this time with all her strength.

"I'm a medical doctor!" she stated in a voice that was close to a shout. "I want to know what's going on here."

Osborne remained frozen in his tracks, like a deer caught in headlights on a highway.

"Sir," Scully informed him, "either you let me in or a lot of people in Washington are going to learn you're conducting some kind of secret quarantine in here. A quarantine that may be above the law. Or quite possibly against it."

Osborne bit his lip. Scully stared into his eyes. Osborne blinked first.

The doctor unlocked and opened the door. But he stood in front of it, continuing to block Scully's entry.

"I'm under strict orders," he warned her.

"So am I," she shot back, advancing so that their faces were no more than inches apart.

"But—," he said.

He was too late. Scully had already pushed past him.

The best he could do was lock the door again. "All that I can tell you is that a flulike illness has spread among some of the prisoners."

"How many are infected?" Scully asked.

"Fourteen men," Osborne said. He had a hard time getting the words out. Then he added, with even more difficulty, "So far."

"Any deaths?" Scully pressed him.

Osborne swallowed hard. "Ten of the fourteen," he finally managed to say.

It was Scully's turn to swallow hard.

Then she took a deep breath and asked, "What are the chances that the men who escaped are infected?"

Osborne could only shake his head. Who knew? He didn't. No one did. They'd have to wait to find out.

That answer was answer enough for Scully.

She whipped out her cell phone and punched Mulder's number.

She could only hope she reached him in time.

Chapter Seven

The phone in Mulder's pocket buzzed.

He was standing at the rest stop watching one of the marshals interview a distraught Anne Tracy.

"Mulder here," Mulder said into the phone.

He heard Scully's urgent voice. "Mulder, it's me. I'm starting to get a picture of what's going on in here."

"What did you find?" Mulder asked.

"There seems to be some kind of deadly disease sweeping the prison population," Scully told him.

"Deadly?" Mulder raised his eyebrows. "How deadly?"

There was a pause. Mulder heard her speak in a muffled voice to someone near her.

Then Scully was back on the phone.

"Well, from what I've seen so far, thirty-six-hours-after-infection deadly."

"Is there a chance the escaped men might be infected?" Mulder asked.

"That's why I called you," Scully said. "The exact nature of this disease and how it spreads is unclear, and so is any danger it poses. Mulder, I urge you to be careful of any contact with them. Or with anyone or anything they have been in contact with."

Mulder thought of the corpse on the rest room floor. The blood on the tile. The rock he and Tapia were looking at now.

He gave a mental shrug. "Thanks for the warning," he said. "Call me as soon as you know anything."

Scully clicked off her phone and put it away. Then she turned to the nervous Dr. Osborne.

"I'd like to inspect the prison infirmary, please," she requested.

"But—," Osborne started to object.

"No *buts* please," Scully cut him off. "As I told you, I have had thorough training as a medical doctor. And I have the authority of a federal agent."

Osborne gave a defeated shrug.

"Come this way," he said. He led her down the corridor, until they reached a large window.

Scully looked through it—and saw the prison infirmary.

It was a large room filled with rows of beds, all of which held patients. Men in protective gear were tending them. The medical equipment they were using looked to be state-of-the-art.

"Please understand that I cannot permit you to enter," Dr. Osborne told her. "It would be entirely too dangerous without the proper attire."

Scully nodded. She was about to ask him where she could get that proper garb. But before she could, she saw two men in protective gear carrying a stretcher down the corridor. A patient lay on the stretcher, enclosed in a clear plastic bubble. Beside them walked another man, in protective gear as well, but with the masked hood off.

The bareheaded man stiffened when he saw Scully.

He waved for the stretcher bearer to enter the infirmary. He went to Dr. Osborne, his face flushed with anger.

"Who is she?" he demanded. "What is the meaning of this?"

"She's with the FBI," Osborne said. His voice quavered nervously.

Ignoring him, the man turned to Scully. "I'm Dr. Auerbach, in charge of operations. I'll have to ask you to leave immediately."

"As Dr. Osborne informed you, I am a federal agent," Scully said. "If you want to see my ID—"

"I don't care who you are or what your business is. I want you out of here right now!" Auerbach shouted at her.

"Not until I get some answers," Scully replied evenly.

Auerbach bristled. "You are in violation of law."

"I'm a federal agent," Scully reminded him.

"Who were you talking to?" Auerbach asked.

"To my partner, who needs to know if the men he's pursuing are infected."

"That information is unavailable," Auerbach declared, not budging an inch.

"Then I want to see charts," Scully insisted. "And I want access to the infirmary."

"You will see what I let you see—when I decide you should see it," Auerbach informed her.

Then he turned to Osborne. "Come with me. I want to discuss certain rules you seem to have forgotten."

With that, he led Osborne away down the corridor and through a door at the far end.

Scully watched the door close behind them. Then she went to the infirmary window again. An attendant inside saw her and moved quickly to lower a shade that cut off her view.

Scully looked around her. She spied a hospital cart in the corridor and went to inspect it.

On top of the cart was a supply of latex gloves and surgical masks.

Scully knew what she needed to do.

Chapter Eight

Elizabeth Zimmer's face was harder than it should have been for a woman in her twenties. Tough times had done that. But her face melted with happiness when she heard the voice on the phone.

"Paul!" she cried in delight, looking like the pretty young woman she was. The baby she held gurgled with pleasure, as if feeling Elizabeth's joy.

"I'm free, baby," Paul told her.

"But how——?" Elizabeth asked, surprised.

"Just listen to me," Paul interrupted. "I'm coming home."

"What are you talking about, honey?" To Elizabeth, it was too good to be true.

"I told you I'd get out and come get you," Paul said. "I told you to trust me."

"Oh, Paul, it's been so long. . . ." Elizabeth didn't even try to contain her excitement. Her sweetheart was coming home.

Paul hung up the phone and left the phone booth. The escaped convict walked across the big parking lot of the gas station where he and Steve had stopped to fuel up. The motor home they had stolen really guzzled gas—not that they planned on paying for it. The lone attendant on duty would soon get a visit from them. Paul figured the day's take would still be in the cash register.

Paul's eyes narrowed as he neared the large white vehicle. It was parked where he had left it, next to the self-service pump.

Funny, Paul thought. *Steve should have moved it by now.* Otherwise the attendant might have looked up from that magazine he was buried in and maybe gotten curious enough to get up and check things out. That greasy-haired kid had to be bored out of his mind. *This dump was in the middle of nowhere, and in the middle of the night it was like a graveyard,* he thought.

When Paul reached the motor home, he saw the gas hose still in the tank. But Steve was nowhere in sight.

Paul thought for a second. He remembered that Steve wasn't feeling so good. They even had to stop once to let him vomit up the food they had found in the vehicle and wolfed down. Steve had probably run to the rest room.

Paul waited a few minutes for Steve to return from his pit stop. Then he headed for the men's room to see what was happening.

He tensed as he went past the brightly lit gas station office. The attendant was no longer there. Paul saw a monkey wrench lying next to a car and picked it up.

The rest room door was open a crack. Paul shoved it open all the way and quietly stepped inside.

The gas station attendant was kneeling on the floor with his back toward Paul. His body blocked Paul's view of the man lying on the floor, but Paul knew who it was. He stepped forward, and the attendant must have heard him.

The young man turned around and said, "Hey Mister, something's wrong with this guy here. He's . . ."

Paul didn't hear anymore. His monkey wrench bashed in the side of the kid's head.

He forgot the attendant completely when he took a look at Steve.

Steve was writhing on the floor in front of a toilet bowl. He was on his back, and Paul saw a huge purple boil swelling on his cheek.

"Don't feel so good," Steve moaned, looking up at his good buddy. "Paul, you gotta help me. I feel like I'm dying. What do you think is the matter with me?"

Paul looked down and scratched his head.

He wished he knew.

But all he knew for sure was what he had to do now.

Get himself and his pal the fastest wheels he could find. And then burn rubber.

Scully entered the basement room and noticed laundry bins stuffed with prison clothing and bedding in front of the incinerator. Piled next to them were figures wrapped in plastic.

Corpses.

Scully pulled on her latex gloves and gave them a yank to draw them skintight. She fitted the surgical mask snugly over her face. Then she carefully cut open one of the body bags.

She recognized the dead man—but only barely. She had been shown Bobby Torrence's photo in her briefing for this assignment— but that picture had been taken when he was healthy. It had not prepared her for the huge, bulging boils that covered Bobby from head to foot.

Scully was using all her medical training not to gag at the sight when a voice behind her made her wheel around.

"You can't be down here," Dr. Osborne snapped at her.

"I need to know what these men have died from," Scully insisted. "You said this was a flulike illness. It's not like any flu I've ever encountered. What are these—"

"Please," Osborne begged, no longer threatening. "The bodies shouldn't be exposed."

"Do all the victims have these boils?" Scully demanded.

Osborne paid no attention. His mind was on a more urgent matter. He set about wrapping the plastic back around Bobby Torrence.

Scully refused to be ignored. As Osborne bent over the corpse, she leaned down to say into Osborne's ear, "You're burning the bodies. *Why?*"

Still Osborne ignored her, as he reached forward to get the last piece of plastic over Bobby's boil-covered face.

As he leaned over, the biggest boil on the dead man's face exploded.

Yellow pus shot up. It hit Osborne, and splattered across his forehead.

For a moment Osborne did not realize what happened.

Then he did.

"*Aghhh!*" came out of his throat.

Then he ran out of the room screaming.

"Dr. Osborne! Wait!" Scully shouted.

But she might as well have been shouting at empty air—or at one of the corpses stacked around her.

Chapter Nine

"Bingo!" Tapia yelled, and pressed down on the accelerator.

"Looks like it," said Mulder, beside him in the car.

In the early morning light they could both see the big white mobile home parked at a gas station down the highway.

Tapia spoke into the car radio. "Get ready for action," he said to the cars behind him. "The vehicle is in the gas station directly ahead. The escapees are probably there as well. We hit that station fast and hard."

Tapia led the way, speeding into the station parking lot and skidding to a stop. The car had barely come to a halt when he was out of it, gun in hand, racing for the parked motor home.

Around him other marshals jumped out of

their cars and swarmed through the station, weapons at the ready.

Tapia kicked open the door to the mobile home and stuck his gun through the doorway.

"Freeze!" he bellowed. "Hands in the air!"

Silence.

Finger on the trigger, he entered.

Nobody at home.

At that moment another marshal kicked open the gas station office.

The lights were on but the office was deserted. In one corner, the door of a safe hung open. The marshal looked inside. It was empty.

Mulder had his own destination. He headed for the men's room, gun in hand. The escapees had used a rest room once before to make a kill. In Mulder's experience, robbers pulled the same stunts over and over again.

Mulder kicked open the men's room door.

He saw a body on the floor.

"We've got a man down!" Mulder shouted from the doorway. Then he entered and knelt for a closer look at the young man whose thick head of hair was soaked with blood.

The victim groaned and stirred.

"He's alive," Mulder told Tapia, who had come to kneel beside him.

The young man groggily tried to sit up.

"Take it easy," Mulder said to him gently. "You'd better not move just yet."

After twenty minutes of gentle probing, the injured victim had told them all he was going to before blacking out.

Mulder went outside to find Tapia.

"The victim's name is Angelo Garza," Mulder told him. "He's got a nice crack on the head, but his memory is intact."

"He's lucky they didn't kill him," Tapia said.

"Lucky for the kid, he's got a lot of hair. It must have helped to absorb the blow," Mulder added.

"He said he found a man lying on the rest room floor," Mulder continued. "From Angelo's description, the man was Steve Tyson. He was in a state of serious suffering. It seems that he was half out of his mind with pain, and has a large, ugly boil on his face."

Mulder paused, his eyes narrowing.

"A boil?" Tapia looked at him questioningly.

"There's an epidemic of some kind in the prison," Mulder told him. "The escapees could have been infected."

Tapia shouted to one of his men, "Eames! Get on the horn. Find out what anyone knows about that."

"Or at least what anyone will tell," Mulder interjected. "The authorities seem reluctant to discuss the nature of the outbreak."

"Whatever the disease is, let's hope it slows the escapees down," said Tapia. "Otherwise we got trouble. They took the kid's keys, got into the safe. They got money, the kid's car, and a firearm he kept in his desk. And they've got a big head start."

"Any guess where they're going?" asked Mulder.

Tapia grimaced. "There are twenty-three possible roads and highways."

"Either of these guys have family they were

close to?" Mulder asked. "Or maybe girlfriends?"

"Wish I could tell you," Tapia explained. "But those records are locked in the prison. Until we can get access to them, we're on our own. For now, it's Smokey and the Bandit."

"If the escapees did have anyone to turn to, they probably tried to call them," Mulder suggested. "You think of that?"

Tapia shrugged.

Mulder pointed to a phone booth at the edge of the gas station parking lot. By the time Tapia nodded his understanding, Mulder was already on his way toward it.

He reached the booth, entered it, and pulled out a notebook and pen. Then he punched in a phone number.

"Atlantic Bell Operator, how may I help you?" said a cheerful female voice.

"I'm a federal agent assisting in the manhunt of two escaped prisoners," Mulder explained. "My badge number is JTT047101111. I need to know the last number dialed from this phone—"

A deafening roar from above drowned out

the operator's reply. Mulder looked through the open door of the booth.

A large yellow helicopter was coming down fast, its rotor blades blowing debris across the parking lot as it landed.

Mulder shouted into the mouthpiece above the thundering noise, "Could you please repeat that number and address?"

With the phone tucked between his head and shoulder, Mulder strained to catch the reply, keeping his eyes on the action as he scribbled down the information.

He saw four men in decontamination gear come running full speed out of the chopper. They raced straight for the gas station rest room, carrying a stretcher covered by a plastic bubble.

In less than a minute, they emerged with Angelo Garza under the bubble. Tapia was screaming at them to stop.

"What's going on here?" he asked. "What are you guys doing here? What the hell is going on here? Who authorized these?"

But they paid no attention to his questions.

Mulder hung up the phone and ran to cut the men off.

He was too late. They were already loading the stretcher into the open bay of the chopper.

Mulder tried to yell over the sound of the helicopter. "What's going on?"

He met Angelo Garza's frightened eyes through the bubble. "Where are they taking me?" the young man asked.

Then the helicopter blades started whirling, lifting the chopper into the air. Swirling gusts of wind hit Mulder like fists. Driven back, he watched the chopper rise and fly off into the bright blue sky.

Near him, Tapia and his men felt just as helpless, stunned by the speed and precision of it all.

Tapia stormed over to Mulder. "Did you order this?"

"No," Mulder answered flatly.

"Then who the devil did?" Tapia demanded.

"I don't know."

"Whatever," said Tapia with a shrug.

Mulder took out his notebook. "I did find out there was a call made from the phone booth two hours ago. I got the number that was called and an address in Dinwiddie County."

Tapia grabbed the notebook and eagerly read, "Nine-two-five August Street. 555-6936."

Chapter Ten

The low brick house at 925 August Street wasn't much, but Elizabeth Zimmer tried to keep it as nice as she could. She wanted a decent place for her baby to grow up in—and for Paul Zimmer to come home to.

She was busy giving the living room a quick dusting when she heard the car outside. She didn't have to wait for the doorbell. She checked to make sure the baby was okay, then she ran out the front door.

She was swept up in Paul's arms. She felt warm and safe for the first time since he was taken off to jail.

Every time she visited him there, he told her he'd get out. He would come for her and the baby, and they'd cut out of here. He had it all planned out. They would go to another country. He'd met a guy in prison who made phony passports. That's all they would need to live happy and free.

Elizabeth hadn't really believed him, though she pretended she did. In fact, she hardly believed him on the phone last night—but she did when he held her tight and whispered, "Told you, baby, here I am."

"I thought you were just fooling!" Elizabeth cried, breathless with joy. "You know, trying to make me feel better."

"I'm gone from that place, sweet thing," Paul assured her. "And they ain't takin' me back."

"I ain't gonna let them," Elizabeth pledged, raising her lips for another kiss.

Just then she heard the baby crying from the house.

"I'm coming, sweetie!" Elizabeth shouted through the screen door. "Daddy's home."

Then she said to Paul, "Let's go inside, honey."

"I got someone with me," Paul told her. He led Elizabeth out to the car, a battered, souped-up Datsun B210 that he had stolen from the gas station.

Inside, she saw a man slumped back in a bucket seat. His head swung from side to side, fighting pain. His eyes were glazed, seeing nothing. And on his cheek, a huge purple boil ballooned.

"This is Steve," Paul said. "He's my pal. He helped me get out. Now we gotta help him."

"What's wrong with him?" Elizabeth asked.

"I don't know," Paul confessed. "And he can't tell me. He's out of it."

Elizabeth reached out and felt Steve's flushed forehead.

"He's burning up."

"Let's get him into the house," Paul said, grabbing his buddy under the armpits and lifting him out of the car.

"But honey . . . the baby . . . what if it's catching . . . ?" Elizabeth asked, hesitating.

"I told you, he's my pal," Paul declared, in a tone Elizabeth knew all too well.

All Elizabeth could do was to run into the house first and get the baby. She moved Paul

Jr. and his crib into a room as far away as she could from the bedroom where Paul carried his sick buddy.

"You keep an eye on Steve," Paul called to her from the bedroom. "I gotta make some calls and get the bus schedules. Soon as we can, we're outta here."

Elizabeth gave the baby a pacifier. "You be good for a couple of minutes, sweetie. Mommy's gotta help a friend."

"Maybe you can get him some aspirin or something," Paul told her when she entered the bedroom. He was already heading out of the room as he spoke.

She sat down on the bed where Steve lay groaning. She felt his forehead again. It was sizzling. She'd try to get some aspirin down his throat, though she didn't expect it would do much. Not as sick as this guy was.

As she started to get up, Steve grabbed her arm.

He looked at her with burning eyes.

"Gotta keep moving," he raved. "Gotta go fast . . . faster . . . faster . . ."

Just then the baby started crying.

Elizabeth tried to break free of his grip. It was like iron.

"Paul, your friend, he's awake!" Elizabeth shouted into the other room. There was no answer. Paul must have been busy on the phone. "Paul . . . come on . . . I gotta go take care of the baby!" she shouted still louder.

"Help me, please!" Steve groaned. "I'm burning up . . . on fire . . . please . . ."

Elizabeth turned to him and leaned over. She tried to think of something to say, something to make him feel better. She opened her mouth, hoping some words would come out.

At that moment, the boil on Steve's face exploded.

The stuff that shot out of it splattered Elizabeth's face and bare arms.

Nasty, icky, disgusting *stuff*.

"Ugghhh!" Elizabeth gasped. Gagging, she fought to keep her lunch down as she ran for the bathroom.

She grabbed the soap and started scrubbing her face and arms. And scrubbing. And scrubbing.

Chapter Eleven

The dead prisoner's face stared up at Scully. He was still lying in the prison incinerator room with the plastic body bag open. Scully gritted her teeth behind her surgical mask and took another look at the boils on his flesh. Then she bent down to read the label on the body bag.

ROBERT TORRENCE. 001. *So Robert Torrence was the first to die*, she thought.

Another thought occurred to her. She went over to a pile of plastic bags that contained the possessions of the dead prisoners. These, too, were slated to be burned.

She went through them with her latex-gloved hands until she found one with Robert Torrence's name on it. Inside were the usual items. A toothbrush. A razor. Soap. A few books. Underwear, socks, shoes. Then she found what she was looking for—something out of the ordinary.

An express delivery package. It was empty, but the name of the delivery service was intact.

Scully pulled out her cell phone. Through information she got the number of the express mail company. She punched it in and gave her FBI badge number to the woman who answered.

"I'm trying to find out who sent a package to Robert Torrence at the Cumberland State Correctional Facility in Virginia," Scully inquired. "Package ID number DDP112148."

"Will you hold on the line while I get the information, or should I call you back?" she asked.

"I'll hold," Scully said.

As she waited, Scully moved as far away as she could from Bobby Torrence. He may be dead, she thought, but another of those boils could burst at any moment. He was a ticking time bomb—like this whole case, in fact.

Then the woman was back on the phone. "The package in question was sent from Wichita, Kansas," she said.

"Did you record the name of the sender?" Scully asked.

Scully's mouth dropped open when she heard the name.

"Would you please double-check that for me?" Scully asked the woman.

The woman confirmed the information.

"Thank you." Scully pressed the DISCONNECT button, then, without hesitating, hit the automatic speed dial for Mulder's number.

Mulder was in a car with three federal marshals speeding down the highway when his cell phone started ringing. He had barely managed to get out his own name when he heard Scully's voice on the other end.

"What do you know about the Pinck Pharmaceutical Company?" Scully asked.

"It's one of the biggest medicinal drug manufacturers in the country," Mulder explained, suddenly curious. "Probably the biggest. Why?"

"They sent a package to a prisoner here who may have been the first to die from the outbreak," Scully informed him.

"Pinck Pharmaceutical did?" asked Mulder. His brow furrowed. "What was in the package?"

"No idea," Scully said. "It was empty. And nobody around here seems eager to fill in the missing blanks."

"Scully, from the description we got, one of the escaped prisoners had a large inflamed boil on his face."

"Sounds like the same thing I'm finding on the victims in here," Scully said, clearly alarmed. "You know what that means, Mulder?"

"Yeah," he replied. "This contagion could spread. From inside the prison to outside. And there are a lot of people outside."

"We need to know more about this disease, Scully," Mulder continued. "How it's transmitted."

Mulder started to say more, but he felt the

car slowing. Looking ahead, he saw that Tapia's car had come to a stop before a low brick house.

"I'm on it," Scully answered.

Scully hung up the phone. She knew what she had to do—she just didn't much feel like doing it.

She went back to Bobby Torrence.

She made sure her surgical mask was on tight. She bent down to look closely into the oozing, raw hole in the skin where the boil had burst.

She saw something in the center. Something small and black. She took out her Swiss Army knife and slid out the tweezers.

Slowly, carefully, she lifted the tiny black object out of the large, open wound.

It was a bug.

For a second it was motionless. Then its feelers began to wiggle in the air.

It was alive.

Elizabeth Zimmer was running into her living room, frantically looking for Paul, when the front door kicked open.

A squad of men came running into her house. Their dark windbreakers and guns marked them as lawmen.

A powerfully built, balding man led them. He screamed at her, "Down on the ground!"

Elizabeth dropped to the floor and lay trembling on her back.

"Hands behind your head!" the man bellowed.

Elizabeth obeyed. She never argued with guns pointed at her. But she managed to lift her head enough to see another man, in a civilian suit, head for the bedroom where Steve lay.

A moment later, Mulder's voice shouted from the bedroom, "We got one dead prisoner in here!"

"And the other?" Tapia shouted back.

"No trace!" Mulder answered. "He's gone!"

Chapter Twelve

Most of the windows of the J. Edgar Hoover Building in Washington, D.C., were dark when Mulder arrived. The guard recognized Mulder and waved him through. It was not the first time that Mulder had shown up after hours at FBI Headquarters. Mulder's odd working hours in his basement office were legendary at the bureau.

Tonight, though, Mulder did not take the elevator down but up—to the office of Assistant Director Walter S. Skinner.

Skinner's outer office was dark, his secretary gone for the day. The door to his inner office was open a crack. A dim sliver of light came through. Mulder pushed the door open.

In the light of a desk lamp, Skinner rose to greet him.

"Come in," Skinner told Mulder. "And please close the door behind you."

"Thank you for seeing me at this hour, sir," Mulder replied, but there was no warmth in his voice.

"What is it, Agent Mulder?" Skinner asked in a weary tone.

"The assignment Agent Scully and I were given," Mulder began. "I believe we've been misled. Possibly deceived."

"Deceived?" Skinner said. "By whom?"

"Whoever originated this case," Mulder responded. "You know that better than I."

"What are you accusing this unknown person of, Agent Mulder?" a voice asked from a darkened corner of the office.

Mulder looked over and saw a man sitting on a couch. His face was in shadow, but Mulder recognized him by the burning end of his eternal cigarette and permanent cloud of smoke that enveloped him.

Mulder had never been able find out the man's name. He simply referred to him as Cancer Man.

Mulder kept a tight hold on his temper. He always had to watch his step with Cancer Man. The man seemed to know just what buttons to push to make Mulder lose it.

"My accusation is quite simple," Mulder answered evenly. "Agent Scully and I were given this assignment without being told that a highly infectious disease was involved."

"What is the exact nature of this disease?" Cancer Man inquired, taking a deep drag on his cigarette.

"It's deadly," Mulder explained. "It kills within thirty-six hours. One of the escaped convicts we were ordered to find was infected. He's dead now.

"The other man may also be infected," Mulder went on, emphasizing his words. "He is now on the loose among the general population."

"Tell me, Agent Mulder, does anyone know how it's communicated? If it's a virus or a bacteria?" Cancer Man asked.

"We know it's already killed over a dozen men," Mulder said sharply. "And it appears to spread very rapidly."

"Then you don't know much, do you, Agent Mulder?" Cancer Man replied. His contempt was as heavy as the smoke he exhaled.

"Why weren't we told the truth about this case?" Mulder demanded.

"We didn't know the truth," Cancer Man responded. "And what we did know would have only slowed you down."

"Innocent people may be infected," Mulder snapped. "What you knew could have prevented that."

"You think so? How?" Cancer Man said. "In 1988, there was an outbreak of hemorrhagic fever in Sacramento, California. The truth would have caused panic. Panic would have cost lives. We controlled the disease by controlling the information."

"You can't protect the public by lying to them," Mulder argued.

Stubbing out his cigarette butt, Cancer Man lit another before answering, "It's done every day."

"Well, I won't be a party to it," Mulder

objected. He turned to Skinner. "What about you? What side are you on?"

Mulder was about to press Skinner harder when Cancer Man's voice cut in, "You're a party to this operation already, Agent Mulder. You can't walk away from it. You can only go forward. How many people are being infected while you stand here not doing your job? Ten, Twenty? What *is* the truth, Agent Mulder?"

"Whatever it is, I'll find it," was the only thing Mulder could say.

Chapter Thirteen

Scully hoped that Mulder was getting closer to the truth than she was. Steel doors continued to isolate her from what was going on at the Cumberland State Correctional Facility.

Outside one of those doors now, through the window she saw men in decontamination suits strapping down a sick prisoner on an examining table. She leaned forward, pressing her nose against the glass.

She did not get to see the rest.

Just then a hand from behind closed like a vise on her shoulder and spun her around. She stared into the face of Dr. Osborne, ghostly pale and dripping with sweat.

"Come with me," he ordered.

"Why? What's going on?" Scully asked.

"Just come with me," Osborne said, his

voice as grave and unyielding as the hand on Scully's shoulder.

Scully didn't argue.

Osborne led her down the hallway to a half-open door. He scanned the corridor to make sure no one had seen them. Then he pulled Scully into a small room and closed the door behind them, locking it.

"What the devil is going on here?" Scully demanded.

Wordlessly, Osborne undid the top buttons of his shirt, pulling it down to expose his neck just above his right collarbone. Scully saw a huge purple-red boil a foot from her face.

"I've been infected," Osborne said.

Despite herself, Scully started to draw back from him.

Osborne smiled grimly. "I don't blame you for wanting to stay away from me. But don't worry. This boil is still in an early stage. It's not ready to erupt just yet."

"We should get you out of here," Scully said.

"Forget it," Osborne said. "They're not letting me out."

"That's outrageous!" Scully exclaimed. "I will personally—"

"They're not letting you out, either," Osborne informed her. "The entire prison is quarantined."

"By what?" The Centers for Disease Control?" Scully asked.

"The CDC has nothing to do with this. It's the company. They're behind everything."

"The company?" said Scully, puzzled. Then it hit her. "Pinck Pharmaceutical? You work for Pinck Pharmaceutical."

Dr. Osborne nodded.

"Then Pinck is behind this outbreak?" Scully asked.

"You might say so."

"How?" Scully demanded.

"We finance investigation of rare species of insects in the rain forests," Osborne said. "Some of them have disease-fighting capabilities worth a fortune to our business. Three months ago, one of our researchers disappeared in Costa Rica."

"Disappeared how?" Scully asked.

"We're not sure," Osborne told her. "We employed the local army to find him, but they could not give positive identification. All we know is that he had sent us some samples of an unusual insect—"

Instantly, Scully pulled out a small specimen bottle from her pocket.

Inside the bottle was a tiny black bug.

Osborne looked at it, his eyes narrowing.

"Where did you get this?" he wanted to know.

"I found it on one of the dead prisoners," Scully told him.

"Faciphaga Emasculata," Osborne explained. "We were interested in it because it secretes an enzyme useful in dilating blood vessels. Such an enzyme would have huge market value."

"Is this what caused the outbreak?"

Osborne shook his head. "No. Not directly."

"What do you mean?" she asked.

"F. Emasculata is a parasitoid." Osborne explained. "It carries a parasite. In this case, a deadly parasite that attacks the immune system. The pustules you've seen are part of the reproductive cycle. They're full of larva. Take a look through the microscope." Osborne directed Scully to a large electromicroscope set up on a lab table. "I took a specimen from my skin right after the accident."

Through the lens Scully saw hundreds of twisting, squirming creatures.

"So the contagion only spreads when the boils erupt and the parasites find a new victim," Scully suggested.

"That's correct, Agent Scully," Osborne confirmed "The parasites burrow under the skin, enter the bloodstream, and begin their work. Even worse is how fast they operate."

Osborne paused and looked at Scully. She knew what that look meant. The thought already had crossed her mind.

"Agent Scully," Osborne spoke softly. "You were there when the boil erupted on me. There is a chance that parasites reached your skin as well. You may already be infected."

Chapter Fourteen

Mulder was in the parking lot of FBI Head-quarters when the cell phone in his pocket sounded.

His hand was on the handle of his car door. He was still fuming at Cancer Man's sneering contempt.

Mulder couldn't help but wonder what kind of people he was working for. Whose side were they on, anyway? And where did that leave him? It was not the first time Mulder had asked himself this question. He had yet to come up with an answer.

His phone sounded again, and he thought of simply letting it ring.

Then he thought of Paul Zimmer—an escaped convict on the loose—and the plague that could sweep through the population like wildfire.

"Mulder." He sighed into the phone.

"Mulder," Scully began. Her voice sounded shaky. "They're enforcing a total quarantine."

"Who are 'they'?" asked Mulder.

"Pinck Pharmaceuticals."

"You're sure?" Mulder seemed skeptical.

"A scientist here told me everything," Scully began. "He works for them."

"How are they involved?"

"They're here cleaning up an experiment that went out of control," Scully continued.

"What kind of experiment?" Mulder asked.

"I'm not sure," Scully said. "But they seem to have been using prisoners as guinea pigs. And that's not all."

"What else?"

"The government, *our* government, has to be in on it," Scully said. "They're helping Pinck with the cover-up. They're keeping it quiet."

"Do you have proof?" Mulder wanted to know.

"Why else would they have the National Guard here? They are protecting Pinck

Pharmaceuticals," Scully asked.

"Scully, listen to me," Mulder told her in a steady voice. "I need to know exactly what happened. The people have to know about this cover-up."

"You mean, tell the public?" asked Scully, incredulous.

"We're dealing with a public health crisis," he pointed out.

"Mulder, we can't leak this," Scully implored. "Not until we know more. The fugitive you're looking for may not even be infected."

"But what if he is?" Mulder demanded.

"Mulder, if this gets out before you catch him, the panic will spread faster than the disease," Scully warned.

"What if someone dies because we kept this whole thing secret?" Mulder asked.

"What if someone dies because we didn't?"

After a long pause, Mulder sighed. He knew Scully was right.

"Look Mulder, there'll be a time for the truth to come out—but this isn't it," she said to him soothingly.

Mulder paused a moment before going on. "Scully, are you okay in there?" he asked.

"I'm fine, Mulder," Scully finally answered. "Look, I want you to worry about one thing only. Capturing that prisoner.

"Take care of yourself, Mulder," she said before clicking off.

Chapter Fifteen

Scully put her phone away and turned to Dr. Osborne. She saw that his shirt was completely soaked through with sweat. *Rising fever*, she thought. *The parasites at work.*

There was fever in his eyes, too, as he looked at her. And fever in his voice.

"If you're not infected, you should leave here immediately," he told her. "Do what you have to, but get out. Pinck will go to any lengths to cover this up."

"And if I am infected?" Scully asked, trying to keep her voice cool.

Osborne shook his head. "You know the answer to that one."

"How do I find out if I'm a carrier?"

"With *these*," Osborne said, pointing to several small plastic containers on a lab table. Each container held a live bug.

"These are bugs that are not now infected by parasites," he explained.

"Which means?"

"It means we can use them to see if any parasites are in your bloodstream," Osborne continued. "Ordinary tests cannot detect the parasites there. These uninfected insects act as incubators. If we let one of them bite you, any parasites that may be present will multiply inside the insect. We will then be able to spot them."

Scully swallowed hard, and held out her bare arm.

"This may sting a bit." With a quick gesture, Osborne placed a plastic container against Scully's forearm. Then he slid the bottom off the container. Scully watched the insect inside explore a patch of her skin with its feelers.

Scully had seen more pleasant sights in her life.

"How long will this take?" she asked as Dr. Osborne taped the plastic box in place. She kept her voice steady, though her stomach was doing cartwheels.

Osborne wiped sweat from his forehead. His hands had begun to tremble.

"Thirty minutes," he told her. "Then another two hours before it reproduces enough for us to detect it."

Scully looked at the bug on her arm.

All she could do was watch. And wait.

"I'd like to see Elizabeth Zimmer alone," Mulder told Tapia. They were in the waiting room of Dinwiddie County Hospital.

"She's in room one-oh-eight. Just show the guard at the door your badge. He'll let you in. I don't think your ID will do you any good with her, though."

Tapia was right. He found Elizabeth in a brightly lit isolation enclosure. When Mulder showed her his badge, she glared at him through the protective plastic shield.

Beneath that angry facade, though, Mulder could see something else, something that Elizabeth could not quite hide.

She was one very scared young woman.

"Elizabeth," he said to her gently, "my name is Fox Mulder. I'm with the FBI. Where did Paul go?"

"I don't know," she said.

"I think you do know," Mulder pressed.

Elizabeth said nothing. Her look said it all. She did not care what Mulder thought.

Until he said, "I also think you know why you're in the hospital."

Suddenly Elizabeth was paying attention to Mulder.

"How are you feeling?" he asked her.

"I'm fine," she snapped bitterly.

"Your husband's friend Steve felt fine, too," Mulder went on. "It didn't take long for that to change."

"You're just trying to scare me," Elizabeth shot back.

"You should be scared," Mulder said softly. "If I were you, I'd be scared, too."

"You're lying," Elizabeth said, a note of desperation in her voice.

"Paul is the one who lied to you," Mulder stated plainly. "His friend had a sickness that could kill not only him but people around him. And if Paul has that sickness as well, a lot of people besides him are going to die."

Elizabeth shook her head. Her eyes narrowed, looking for a reason not to believe what Mulder said.

"If that's true, how come it's not on TV?" she demanded. "How come they're not telling everybody?"

Her eyes challenged Mulder to come up with an answer.

"That's not my decision," he told her.

"Well, whose decision is it?" Elizabeth's words seared into him. "You knew about it and you didn't say anything. Why should I tell the truth if you won't?"

It was a good question.

Mulder wished he could answer it.

He wished he could say more than, "Elizabeth, Paul is out there somewhere. I have to find him. Now you can help me. Or not. It's up to you."

Chapter Sixteen

"Why did you decide to tell me the truth?" Scully asked Dr. Osborne.

Osborne lay in a hallway on a stretcher with a plastic bubble. He had collapsed while waiting to test the bug that had fed on Scully.

Two men in protective gear saw him fall to the corridor floor. They asked no questions and wasted no time. While Scully watched helplessly, they strapped Osborne onto the stretcher and closed the bubble over him. Then they left him there, vanishing into another corridor.

Osborne was too weak to struggle against the straps that held him down. He had barely enough strength to talk. Scully had to lean forward to catch his words through the bubble.

"This isn't a secret I want to take to the grave," he wheezed. "People have a right to know the danger we've put them in."

He paused, panting. Then he gathered enough energy to say, "The poisons, they're moving to my brain. Just like they did with the prisoners."

"Is there anything I can do for you?" Scully asked.

Osborne shook his head. Then with great difficulty managed to gasp out, "You have to complete the test . . . if you're not sick, you have to get out of here. You must get the word out . . . what happened here . . ."

Osborne paused for breath again. Scully saw his eyes filming over.

"How can I prove it?" Scully asked urgently, while he still could answer.

"I don't know," said Osborne, his voice a fading moan. "But if you don't, it'll happen again. Don't believe for a second that this is an isolated incident."

That was as far as he could go. His head

fell backward, eyes rolling upward. He was gasping now like a fish out of water.

Scully looked at him. It was her turn to shake her head. There was nothing she could do for him. Except to follow his last wish.

She glanced at her watch. It was time to examine the engorged insect. If parasites were in the blood, they would be swarming there by now. Then Scully would find out whether she shared Osborne's fate.

Scully went to Osborne's lab. The bug lay dead in an airtight container. Its belly was swollen with blood. Her blood.

Scully opened the container. With fine tweezers, she inserted a thin tube into the bulging abdomen. Using a suction device, she drew blood into a test tube.

Slowly, carefully, Scully put a dab of the blood on a glass slide. She slid the slide under a high-power microscope.

She paused and took a deep breath, as if getting up the nerve to jump into icy water.

Then she looked into the microscope.

She saw—nothing.

Nothing but blood cells—not a parasite in sight.

She started breathing again.

She walked quick-step out of the lab and down the corridor to give Osborne the good news—while he still could hear it.

He was gone.

Scully broke into a full run. She raced through the corridors, heading for the prison infirmary.

She reached the infirmary door and pounded on it.

"A new patient, I have to see him," she said to the man who opened it. She shoved her badge in front of his plastic face mask. "He had to be taken here within the last fifteen minutes. I'm sure you know him. He's one of your people. Dr. Osborne."

"He's not here, " the man said.

"Then where is he?" Scully demanded.

The man answered by closing the door in Scully's face.

Scully swallowed hard. She had a feeling

that she knew the answer—and knew where to find Osborne. A sinking feeling.

She jogged through more corridors, past more man in decontamination suits. Then she went down steel stairs and opened the door of the incinerator room.

The room was filled with men in decontamination suits furiously shoving corpses into the furnace, along with their belongings.

By now the huge pile of dead bodies was down to a few.

Soon there would be none.

Scully spotted a man she recognized— the one who called himself Dr. Auerbach. As when she first had met him, he wore no mask. Auerbach seemed at home with deadly danger.

She stormed up to him.

"What are you doing?" she demanded.

"The infected bodies and other materials are being destroyed according to standard Centers of Disease Control procedure," he told her. His response sounded like the message on an answering machine.

"You don't work for the CDC," Scully accused him.

"Really?" Auerbach seemed surprised. "What makes you think that, if I may ask?"

"Dr. Osborne told me everything," Scully continued. "Where is he? What have you done with him?"

Ignoring her question, Auerbach told her, "Believe me, Agent Scully, what is being done here is necessary for the good of all concerned."

"We'll leave that up to others to decide," Scully replied.

Auerbach spun around abruptly. "Look, Agent Scully, Dr. Osbourne is dead. And no on in thei room will back up your story. Just be glad this thing is under control."

Auerbach turned to two of his men and pointed to the last remaining corpse. The men picked it up and fed it into the flames.

Scully saw its face as it went into the furnace.

Silently, she said good-bye to Osborne.

And with him, she said good-bye to her last hope of ever making anyone outside believe that the unbelievable was happening.

It was all up to Mulder now.

Chapter Seventeen

Mulder left Elizabeth Zimmer's room and found Tapia where he had left him.

"He's at the Clarksville bus station," Mulder said. "He's taking the ten o'clock bus to Toronto. She was supposed to be with him."

Tapia looked up at a wall clock. It read a little past nine. He frowned and said, "The station is more than a half hour from here, even if we do ninety."

"Let's get going, then," Mulder said.

"It'd be cutting it too close," Tapia said. He turned and shouted across the room to a marshal sipping coffee. "Get on the phone to the Clarksville police. Tell them to get to the bus station and grab Zimmer. Tell them to use every man they've got."

"*No!*" Mulder protested. The local cops don't know what they're dealing with. If Paul Zimmer is sick, he could infect them. After that, who knows how fast and far this plague could spread? What we need is risk control. We have to isolate him."

Tapia thought for a moment. Then he nodded reluctantly.

The bus company had trained Tina Andrews to give a friendly smile to travelers who came to her ticket counter. But it was hard to smile at a man with long dirty hair, a ragged beard, a nasty-looking boil on his face, and a crazy look in his eyes. Especially when he kept coughing practically in her face.

"One way to Toronto," the bearded man said between coughs. He shoved bills at her. Tina usually didn't think of money as dirty— but she picked up these bills only because it was her job. She gave him his ticket and his change and waited impatiently for him to go away.

But he stayed planted in front of her. He had a question.

"You sell any tickets to a blond woman with a kid?" he asked.

"No sir," Tina said, barely able to unclench her teeth. She had given up even trying to smile.

But the man wasn't looking at her. When he spoke, it was to himself. "Can't wait around for them. Gotta get going. Gotta get out of here."

With relief Tina watched him finally walk away. He seemed to half trip over his own feet as he hurried toward where the Toronto bus waited.

Tina turned to her next customers. A woman with a boy, about twelve, Tina judged.

"Hurry up, Mom," the boy urged. "I don't want that bus to leave without me."

"Don't worry, Jason, you have plenty of time," his mother told him.

The mother turned to Tina and said, "A child's ticket to Toronto."

Jason tugged impatiently at her coat, and the woman said to Tina, "He's so excited. He's going to visit his uncle."

"First time all alone?" Tina asked, with a genuine smile. "That is exciting."

Jason shouldered his duffel bag and headed for the bus.

"Thanks, and bye now," the mother said to Tina, and turned and hurried after her son.

"Don't you come aboard with me," Jason told her when they reached the bus. "I can give the driver the ticket all by myself."

"Just a kiss for the road," his mother begged, and bent down and gave him a peck on the cheek.

"Come on, people'll think I'm a baby," Jason objected, pulling away from her embrace.

His mother smiled at him. She still couldn't resist calling after him as he boarded the bus, "Be careful!"

Jason wasn't listening. He handed the bus driver the ticket and marched down the aisle.

He was halfway to the rear when a big hand reached out and grabbed him.

He stared at a sweating, bearded face with the nastiest purple-red boil he had ever seen protruding from one side.

"What time is it, kid?" the face demanded.

Gulping, Jason looked at his watch.

"T-twenty to t-ten," he stammered.

"Time to get this show on the road," Paul Zimmer growled, releasing the boy and sinking back in his seat.

Why didn't the bus start moving? Paul raged to himself.

As if this were going to take him away from the pain in his guts and fever in his brain.

Chapter Eighteen

Mulder looked around the bus station. The scene was a nightmare for an agent of the law. A milling crowd of travelers packed the place.

Mulder looked at the crew of federal marshals walking through the bus station. They were good at their job, skilled at stealth. Nobody was paying any attention to them.

Mulder headed over to the ticket counter, and asked about the bus heading for Toronto.

The clerk gave him a big smile. "You're in luck, sir. You can just catch the bus. It's running a little late today—but I'm sure the driver will make up the lost time on the way."

Mulder pulled a photo of Paul Zimmer from his coat pocket and held it up for the woman to see. "Have you seen this man?" he asked.

The smile faded from the woman's face as she nodded her head.

"He bought a ticket just a few minutes ago," she told Mulder. "He was pretty strange-looking."

Mulder headed over to where Tapia stood directing his men.

"He's here on the bus to Toronto. And he's infected," Mulder told him.

Just then his cell phone rang. "Mulder."

"Mulder, I think everything here is under control," said Scully.

Mulder sensed nervousness in her voice. "Are you okay, Scully?"

"Yeah. Have you found the second prisoner?"

"He's heading for Toronto," Mulder said.

Scully was shocked. "He's alive? Listen to me, Mulder. Everything here has been destroyed. Any evidence of a cover-up has been incinerated. That prisoner is the last man who could possibly tell us who the conspirators are.

"Mulder was uncertain. "He's infected. He's going to die."

Scully wouldn't back down. "If you want the truth, Mulder, he's going to have to make a statement."

Mulder hung up. He looked around. Tapia had his men positioned all around the bus, ready to move in.

"Hold your men back," he told Tapia.

"*What?*" Tapia looked confounded.

"I'm getting on that bus," Mulder told him.

"You're crazy," Tapia said. "You don't have to play hero. We got the situation under control. The bus isn't going anywhere."

"That's what I'm afraid of," Mulder continued. "You've got other passengers aboard. Paul Zimmer will panic at the first sight of an armed man coming through the door. He panics, and innocent people could die. The guy is a killer, remember. Even worse, he *likes* to kill. Plus, he has nothing left to lose."

Tapia opened his mouth to argue, then wordlessly closed it. Finally, he said, "Okay. So what do you want to do?"

"I board the bus, take the seat behind our man," Mulder explained. "I put my gun to his head and make an announcement for the passengers to clear the bus."

Tapia thought a moment. Then he shrugged and said, "Okay, it's your call."

"Here goes," Mulder said, heading for the bus.

"Please take your seat, sir," the driver said as Mulder handed him his ticket.

But Mulder remained standing beside the driver's seat.

"There was supposed to be a man who got on this bus—" Mulder began.

"Sir, I've got a schedule to keep. Now please sit down or I'll have to ask you to get off."

Mulder had no choice but to slide into a seat directly behind the driver.

"Take your key out of the ignition and turn around slowly," he said into the driver's ear.

The driver turned around. His face was flushed with anger. "What's the problem, mister?" he demanded.

"I'm an FBI agent," Mulder said, taking a photo from his pocket. "I need to know if this man boarded this bus."

The driver looked at the photo and nodded.

"Yeah," he whispered. He looked past Mulder toward the rear of the bus. "That's him right back there."

Mulder turned around sharply in his seat. He saw a big man coming out of the bathroom at the back of the bus.

The man was weaving, and he grabbed the back of a seat for balance. His face was sweating and blotched red with rashes. A huge purple-red boil swelled on his cheek.

Mulder saw he had to scrap his original plan. His mind raced to come up with another.

Paul Zimmer did not give him the time.

Paul had been on the wrong side of the law all his life. One of the lessons of that life was how to spot the law at a glance.

His eyes met Mulder's. Instantly Paul yanked a pistol from his waistband.

All Mulder could do was go for his own weapon as he jumped to his feet.

"Federal agent! Drop your gun!" he shouted above the screams of the passengers.

But dropping his gun was the last thing that Paul had in mind. Instead he grabbed the first person within reach—a terrified twelve-year-old boy whose first trip alone could well be his last.

Chapter Nineteen

Tapia stood on another bus, a full twenty feet from the Toronto bus. But looking in through the window, he could see the action unfolding inside.

Tapia saw Mulder standing rigid, one arm extended with a gun pointed at Paul Zimmer.

Tapia saw Paul aiming his gun at Mulder with one hand. The other arm had a choke hold on the terrified boy who had become a human shield.

Tapia yelled into his walkie-talkie to all the federal marshals in the bus station. "Plan A is down the tube! Get ready to move in when I give the word!"

Tapia was praying he would not have to say that word. It could spell death for a lot of innocent people.

Let's see if you're as good as you think you are, Agent Mulder, Tapia thought. His hand on his gun, he peered at the bus window as though it were a grimy TV screen.

Inside the bus, Mulder's finger was on the trigger, his body tensed. "Let the boy go, Paul."

Paul Zimmer kept his hold on the boy, his gun leveled at Mulder. "Move this bus!" he shouted. Then he paused, panting. His yell had taken something out of him. He felt like he was starting to run on empty—but still had enough strength to pull a trigger.

"You've got two dozen U.S. marshals out there, Paul," Mulder told him. "How far do you think you're gonna get?"

Paul looked out the window. He saw the men with guns drawn surrounding the bus.

"Please, mister, I can't breathe," he heard the boy whimper. Paul realized he must have tightened his grip. He loosened his choke hold only slightly, allowing the frightened boy air enough to start crying. But now it was Paul who was having trouble breathing.

With his gun pointed at Mulder, he gasped, "I'm dying, ain't I?"

"The question is, how many people are you going to take with you?" Mulder wanted to know.

"It's the same thing that killed Steve, right?" Paul wheezed, fighting waves of dizziness washing over him, each one greater than the last.

"That's right, Paul," Mulder told him.

"What is this thing I got?" Paul asked.

"A disease that spreads like wildfire," Mulder said to him. "You were infected in prison."

"Bobby Torrence," said Paul. "It's what he had."

"And now Elizabeth may have it," Mulder went on. "Maybe even your son. How many more people do you want to get it?"

A memory flashed through Paul's brain like a fireball. "It came from that package in Bobby's cell, didn't it?" he demanded.

"You saw a package?" Excitement rose in Mulder's voice.

"What the devil was in it?" Paul cried—and screamed in pain. He felt a knife going

109

through his guts. He let go of the crying kid as he clutched his stomach.

But his gun stayed in his other hand.

Jason was too scared to move. The boy stayed frozen with fear, staring up at the big crazy man's face and the boil that looked ready to pop like a balloon.

Slowly, Mulder inched toward Paul, gun at the ready.

Without taking his eyes off Paul, he told the busload of people, "Okay, folks, everybody off."

By now he was only a few feet from Paul and the wavering barrel of Paul's gun.

"It's okay, kid," Mulder said gently to Jason, while locking eyes with Paul. "It's okay. Just move away from him. Go on."

His voice was enough to break the hold of terror. Jason slid away from Paul, who did not even seem to notice him. The boy pushed past Mulder, who made room for him in the narrow aisle. Then Jason tore out of the bus as if running for his life—right into the arms of his mother, who had been waiting out of sight.

Meanwhile, Mulder had only one question in his mind.

"Paul, what was in the package?" he asked. "The package in Bobby Torrence's cell?"

By now Paul's gun had drooped to his side. His body quaked with pain. He shook his head in a desperate effort to clear it.

"What was in it, Paul?" Mulder asked urgently. Time was running out. *"What was in that package?*

"A pharmaceutical company was using you as a guinea pig. If you tell me what was in that package, I'll make sure they don't get away with it. Come on, Paul, you remember. Tell me."

Paul lifted his head. For a moment, his eyes cleared. He opened his mouth to speak.

But before he could get a word out, a bullet shattered the bus window and buried itself in his brain.

Mulder looked down at the sightless eyes of the dead prisoner on his face. On his face, the boil looked bigger than ever. But the only thing Mulder could see was a dead end to his investigation.

He barely felt the two hands that gripped his shoulders from behind.

He was not surprised to see that a pair of men in decontamination gear had come up behind him.

He did not put up a fight when they pulled him away from the corpse and hustled him off the bus.

Still in shock, he stood with those men on either side of him and watched more of them swarm into the bus, fully equipped to clean up the mess.

The danger was over.

The case was over.

But Mulder had something to say about it.

Chapter Twenty

Mulder did not mince words with Walter Skinner in the assistant director's inner office.

"Robert Torrence was Patient Zero—the first prisoner to die from the disease," Mulder began. "Just before he became sick, he received a package from Pinck Pharmaceuticals. They orchestrated this entire thing to avoid years of government trials in order to get their drug on the market."

"Why are you telling me this, Agent Mulder?" asked Skinner, as he put down the tube containing the dead bug Agent Mulder had handed him.

"Because I wanted you to hear it from me," Mulder informed his boss, "before you read it in the papers."

Skinner seemed to come fully awake for

the first time. He gave Mulder a sharp look. His voice was cutting. "If you're thinking of talking about this to the media, I advise you to think again."

"The public has a right to know what happened at Cumberland," Mulder insisted. "So that it doesn't happen some other place, some other time."

Skinner's thin lips curled in a sneer. "And you're going to prove this elaborate conspiracy with what?" he said. "An empty package and a dead insect?"

Mulder opened his mouth, then closed it.

Before he could speak, Skinner advised, "Leave it alone, Agent Mulder. The epidemic was contained. The threat is over."

"Eighteen people are dead," Mulder pointed out. "And if you're helping cover up the truth behind those deaths—you're as guilty as Pinck is."

Skinner did not flinch at Mulder's accusing stare. His mouth tightened. "Agent Mulder, you really have no idea who you're dealing with, do you?"

"I thought I was dealing with you," Mulder said, his eyes still fixed on his superior.

Before Skinner could respond, someone knocked on the door.

"Yes," Skinner called out.

The door opened and Scully entered. Ignoring Skinner, she spoke directly to Mulder. "We can't prove a thing, Mulder. They made sure of that."

"What are you talking about?" Mulder could already feel a chill.

"I just got a fax from Costa Rica," Scully told him. "It's a report on the missing scientist who discovered the bug. His name was Robert Torrence."

"Robert Torrence," repeated Mulder. "Are you saying what I think you are, Scully?"

Scully nodded grimly. "The same name as the prisoner. It was their insurance against anyone finding out about their project," Scully explained. "If the contents of the package were discovered, Pinck could claim it was a mailing error. Pinck would claim that the express company delivered it to the wrong Robert Torrence."

"They had other insurance on top of that," Mulder said, a light going on in his mind.

"What do you mean?" Scully asked.

Mulder spoke not to Scully but to Skinner. "That's why we were assigned to the case, isn't it?"

Skinner didn't answer. He looked at Mulder coldly, his glasses glinting like ice.

"Pinck wanted to make sure its secrecy was airtight," Mulder reasoned. "It chose to use us to look for any holes in the cover-up. If we did manage to stumble onto anything, Pinck could then make sure it was covered up for good. As for us, we could be counted on to follow orders—or else lose our reputations by making accusations we could not prove. The bureau would not even have to fire us. Just ignore us."

"You never had a chance, Agent Mulder," Skinner told him. "For every step you take, they're three steps ahead of you."

"What about you?" Mulder wanted to know. "Where do you stand in all this?"

"I stand right on the line that you keep crossing," Skinner replied.

Before he could say more, Scully put her hand on his shoulder.

"Come on, Mulder," she said to him. "Let's go."

Mulder's shoulders slumped.

Wordlessly, he went with Scully to the door. He opened it and let her go out first.

Just before he followed her, Skinner's voice from behind stopped him.

"Agent Mulder, I'm saying this as a friend. Watch your back. This is just the beginning."

Mulder did not look back as he left the room.

His pace quickened as he caught up with Scully, and side by side they headed where they were always headed.

In search of the truth.

Don't miss the next X-Files
Young Adult book:

Regeneration
by
Everett Owens

The Pittsburgh city hospital ambulance
crested a hill, its pulsing lights and shrill
siren cutting through the night sky. The
EMT behind the wheel, Michele Wilkes,
maneuvered the ambulance through the
traffic, swerving left then right. Despite the
noise and action around her, Wilkes's eyes
never left the road—a discipline her years
on the job had made instinctive. This late
on a Friday night, she knew she had to be
especially careful. Wilkes pulled her radio
microphone off its rack and switched it on.

"We're en route with a male cardiac, age

sixty-two. Estimated time of arrival, twelve minutes," she said, keeping the message short.

The dispatcher responded in kind.

"Copy, ETA in twelve. Crash unit standing by."

Wilkes allowed herself a glance in the rearview mirror.

"How's he looking, Leonard?"

Wilkes's senior partner, Leonard Betts, was hunched over an elderly black man in the back of the ambulance, simultaneously checking his heartbeat with a stethoscope and a digital heart monitor.

"He's up to his ass in alligators," Betts answered calmly.

Just as he spoke, the monitor emitted a series of short, piercing beeps. The patient gasped loudly, then began gulping for air. Wilkes could hear the monitor going crazy.

"Is he going into arrest?" she shouted.

Ignoring the question, Betts pulled off the stethoscope and put his ear to the man's chest. Satisfied with what he heard, Betts called back to Wilkes. "No, he's not."

Betts reached back into a drawer and pulled out a large hypodermic syringe. Shucking its plastic sleeve and removing the safety tip, Betts jabbed it into the man's windpipe. Instantly, air whistled out through the barrel, and the monitor resumed a steady rhythm. The patient's breathing returned to normal.

Wilkes heard the monitor's calm beeping from the cab and wondered what had just happened.

"What'd you do?" she asked her partner.

Moving efficiently, Betts taped down the syringe. He remained vigilant as he briefed Wilkes.

"Aspirated his chest," he explained. "He has a tension pneumothorax pressing on his heart. It just looked like a cardiac."

Wilkes shook her head, quietly impressed. It never ceased to amaze her that, no matter how dire the situation, Leonard sounded like he was treating a stubbed toe.

"Nice catch," she said, keeping her eyes on the road. "How did you know?"

Betts stared hard at his unconscious patient, looking the man over as if he could almost see through the skin. Finally, he murmured, "Because he's dying of cancer. It's eaten through one lung already."

Wilkes was keenly aware of the equipment available to EMTs in an ambulance. There was no way Leonard could tell this at this point.

"How do you know, Leonard?" she shook her head in wonder.

But Betts didn't answer. He continued to stare into the man's chest. Wilkes turned her head to look back at him for a moment. She wanted to know how he did it, how he always knew ahead of time what doctors at the hospital would confirm hours later. With her head turned, she didn't notice the stoplight ahead of her change from green to red.

The sound of a car horn caused Wilkes to whip her head around. The tow truck's headlights caught the side of her face an instant before the vehicle plowed into her. The violence of the crash shattered metal and flesh like a bomb blast. The ambulance, which had been cruising north, was slammed sideways by the truck, sending it sliding in a shower of broken glass before it crashed into a streetlamp that buckled halfway up. The top section of the streetlamp teetered, then fell down onto the wreckage, illuminating the cab of the tow truck where the driver lay slumped over the wheel, his horn still blaring.

Dazed but conscious, Wilkes pushed the ambulance door open and stumbled out. Blood dripped onto her uniform from a wound on her forehead. She steadied herself by holding on to the mangled door of the ambulance.

"Leonard?" she called out, but there was no answer. Other than the tow truck's horn, the deserted downtown street was quiet as a tomb.

Wilkes picked her way to the back of the ambulance and found the back doors hanging wide open. Nervously, she looked inside, where she discovered the patient lying dead, strapped to a blood-spattered gurney that had flipped over on its side. The heart monitor showed a blue flatline shimmering across its screen. All the medical equipment—the bandages, bottles, pumps, IV bags—had been thrown around the compartment by the impact. But Wilkes still didn't see her partner.

"Leonard!" she yelled.

She turned from the wreckage and scanned the scene. Eventually her eyes fell on a pair of legs stretched out along the sidewalk thirty or forty feet away. A row of newspaper racks concealed the body from the waist up. Wilkes staggered toward the limbs, ducking underneath a utility pole cable, and making her way around the racks. As she did, the rest of the body came into view.

Most of it, anyway.

A wave of nausea hit Wilkes, and she had to cover her mouth to keep from vomiting. She stumbled, then braced herself against one of the newspaper racks and forced herself to look again. Leonard Betts's blue-and-white uniformed body sprawled before her, lying stomach-down in a pool of blood that spurted from the stump of his neck.

"Oh, God. Leonard!" Wilkes cried, her body shuddering helplessly.

Then she saw it, just a few feet away, lodged between a car tire and the curb. Leonard Betts's eyes, frozen open, stared back at her from his severed head.